Cabbage tree and sheep in the Mangawharariki Valley south of Taihape.

Cabbagebaum und Schafe im Tal von Mangawharariki, südlich von Taihape.

Des palmistes et des moutons dans la vallée de Mangawharariki au sud de Taihape.

Arbol-repollo y ovejas en el Valle de Mangawharariki al sur de Taihape.

THE BEAUTY
OF
NEW ZEALAND

Photographs by Warren Jacobs

NH
KOWHAI

NORTH ISLAND

Three Kings Islands
Cape Reinga
North Cape
Te Hapua
Great Exhibition Bay
Pukenui
Karikari Peninsula
Kaitaia
Mangonui
Ninety Mile Beach
Kaeo
Bay of Islands
Tauroa Point
Kerikeri
Russell
Kawakawa
Poor Knights Is
Hokianga Har
Hikurangi
Maungaturoto
Kaikohe
WHANGAREI
Dargaville
Ruawai
Maungaturoto
Little Barrier I
GREAT BARRIER ISLAND
Kaipara Har
Wellsford
Warkworth
Hauraki Gulf
Helensville
Orewa
Great Mercury I
Coromandel
COROMANDEL PENINSULA
Takapuna
Whitianga
AUCKLAND
Manurewa
Papakura
Thames
Whangamata
Mayor I
Manukau Har
Papatoetoe
Waiuku
Whangamata
Pukekohe
White I
Waikato R
Te Kauwhata
Waihi
Mayor I
Cape Runaway
Katikati
Motiti I
Hicks Bay
Ngaruawahia
Raglan
HAMILTON
TAURANGA
BAY OF PLENTY
Te Araroa
East Cape
Te Aroha
Te Puke
Edgecumbe
Te Kaha
Morrinsville
Cambridge
WHAKATANE
Ruatoria
Kawhia
Te Awamutu
Matamata
Opotiki
Albatross point
Putaruru
ROTORUA
Kawerau
Tokomaru Bay
Otorohanga
Tokoroa
Murupara
Tolaga Bay
Te Kuiti
Mangakino
Mt Tarawera
Gisborne
Mokau R
Mokau
Mangakino
Young Nicks Head
NORTH TARANAKI BIGHT
Benneydale
Ohura
Wairoa
Waitara
Taumarunui
Lake Taupo
Taupo
Rangitaiki
Tuai
NEW PLYMOUTH
Inglewood
National Park
Turangi
MAHIA PENINSULA
Cape Egmont
Mt Taranaki/Mt Egmont
2518
Stratford
Mt Ruapehu
2797
Ohakune
Waiouru
HAWKE BAY
Portland I
Opunake
Eltham
Raetihi
HASTINGS
NAPIER
Manaia
Hawera
Waverley
Mangaweka
Tikokino
Havelock North
Cape Kidnappers
SOUTH TARANAKI BIGHT
Patea
Hunterville
Takapau
Waipawa
Waipukurau
WANGANUI
Marton
Dannevirke
Bulls
Feilding
Woodville
Porangahau
Rangitikei R
PALMERSTON NORTH
Pahiatua
Cape Turnagain
Manawatu R
Shannon
Eketahuna
Levin
Pongaroa
Foxton
Kapiti I
Otaki
Waikanae
Masterton
Castlepoint
Paraparaumu
Carterton
Porirua
Greytown
Martinborough
Lower Hutt
WELLINGTON
Cape Palliser

SOUTH ISLAND

Cape Farewell
Farewell Spit
GOLDEN BAY
Collingwood
D'URVILLE ISLAND
Cape Farewell
Takaka
TASMAN BAY
KARAMEA BIGHT
Karamea
Motueka
Havelock
Picton
Little Wanganui
Richmond
NELSON
COOK STRAIT
Wakefield
Blenheim
Granity
Murchison
St Arnaud
Seddon
Westport
Cape Foulwind
Tapuae-o-Uenuku
2885
Clarence
Cape Campbell
Punakaiki
Reefton
Clarence River
Kaikoura
Runanga
Lewis Pass
Hanmer Springs
Kaikoura Peninsula
Greymouth
Kumara
Otira
Culverden
Walau River
Hokitika
Arthurs Pass
Hawarden
Ross
Cheviot
Harihari
Amberley
PEGASUS BAY
Rangiora
Franz Josef Glacier
Whataroa
Kaiapoi
Waimakariri River
Fox Glacier
Springfield
Darfield
CHRISTCHURCH
Mt Cook
3754
Lincoln
Lyttelton
Haast River
Mount Cook
Mt Somers
Akaroa
BANKS PENINSULA
Haast
Methven
Hoast Pass
Lake Tekapo
Ashburton
Jackson Head
Geraldine
Rakaia River
Ashburton River
Fairlie
Twizel
Temuka
Rangitata River
Awarua Point
Mt Aspiring
3027
Lindis Pass
Timaru
CANTERBURY BIGHT
Milford Sound
Omarama
Waimate
Milford Sound
Wanaka
Kurow
George Sound
Glenorchy
Tarras
Maheno
Oamaru
Homer Tunnel
Arrowtown
Cromwell
Waitaki River
SECRETARY I
Queenstown
Ranfurly
Hampden
Dagg Sound
Te Anau
Alexandra
Kingston
Middlemarch
Palmerston
Doubtful Sound
Roxburgh
Waikouaiti
Manapouri
Mossburn
Lumsden
Lawrence
Port Chalmers
OTAGO PENINSULA
Dusky Sound
Ohai
Tapanui
Milton
DUNEDIN
Nightcaps
Gore
Clinton
Balclutha
Winton
Mataura
Kaitangata
Clutha River
Tuatapere
INVERCARGILL
Owaka
FOVEAUX STRAIT
Riverton
Bluff
Chaslands Mistake
Solander I
Codfish I
Ruapuke I
Halfmoon Bay (Oban)
STEWART ISLAND

INTRODUCTION

To the rest of the world, New Zealand is a remote group of islands lying not all that far north of the Antarctic Circle. Therein lies its appeal. Even in this age of jet travel, New Zealand remains relatively removed from the stresses and strains of global activity.

It is New Zealand's spectacular and unspoiled landscape that entices visitors—its mountains and lakes, forests and fiords. Sparsely populated areas abound for enthusiasts of outdoor pursuits. Opportunities to partake of healthy endeavours in superb surroundings are numerous, from the highly adventurous to gentle walks amongst lush forest and tranquil alpine lakes.

New Zealand's cities and scenic destinations are equally diverse and life through town and countryside alike moves at a comfortable pace. The beauty of New Zealand is an experience to be enjoyed and remembered.

Für die übrige Welt besteht Neuseeland aus einer abgelegenen Inselgruppe, die nicht allzuweit nördlich des südlichen Polarkreises gelegen ist. Aber gerade darin liegt ihr Reiz. Selbst im Zeitalter der Düsenflugzeuge ist Neuseeland von den globalen Anspannungen und Anforderungen dieser Welt verschont geblieben.

Es sind Neuseelands spektakuläre und unberührte Landschaften, die die Besucher anziehen—Gebirgs- und Seenlandschaften, ausgedehnte Waldgebiete und majestätische Fjorde, dünn besiedelte Gegenden, die ideal für Freizeitsportler und Naturenthusiasten geeignet sind, und die vielfältigen Möglichkeiten, an naturverbundenen und abenteuerlichen Aktivitäten in herrlicher Umgebung teilzunehmen.

Neuseelands Städte und landschaftliche Anziehungspunkte sind gleichermaßen mannigfaltig, und sowohl das Stadtleben als auch der ländliche Lebensstil in Neuseeland bewegen sich im eher gemütlichen Tempo. Die Schönheit Neuseelands stellt ein Erlebnis dar, das man genießen und in Erinnerung behalten sollte.

Pour le reste du monde, la Nouvelle-Zélande est considérée comme une groupe d'îles isolées situé au nord du cercle antarctique. Mais c'est ce qui la rend attirante. Bien que dans l'ère des avions à réaction, la Nouvelle-Zélande est épargnée des exigences et des tensions de ce monde.

C'est son paysage spectaculaire et vierge qui attire les visiteurs—ses montagnes et ses lacs, ses vastes forêts et ses fjords majestueux, ses régions peu peuplées idéales pour les fervents de sports et de nature et qui offrent la possibilité de s'adonner à des activités de plein air et d'aventure dans un environnement maginifique.

Les villes de la Nouvelle-Zélande sont tout aussi diverses que ses coins touristiques, et la vie citadine aussi bien que le style de vie rural évoluent plutôt à un rythme débonnaire. La beauté de la Nouvelle-Zélande représente une aventure que l'on devrait savourer et en garder le souvenir.

Para el resto del mundo, Nueva Zelanda es un remoto conjunto de islas situadas no mucho más allá al norte del Círculo Antártico. Ahí reside su atractivo. Incluso en ésta la era del transporte aéreo, Nueva Zelanda se mantiene relativamente alejada del estrés y las tensiones de la actividad global.

Es el paisaje de Nueva Zelanda, espectacular y aún en su estado natural el que seduce a los visitantes- sus montañas y lagos, sus bosques y fiordos. Abundan las areas escasamente pobladas para aquellos entusiastas de las actividades al aire libre. Las oportunidades de tomar parte en saludables aventuras con espléndidos escenarios son numerosas, desde las excursiones a pie más atrevidas a las más moderadas entre exuberante bosque y tranquilos lagos alpinos.

Las ciudades de Nueva Zelanda y los destinos pintorescos son igualmente diversos, y la vida a través de la ciudad y el campo transcurre a un ritmo apacible. La belleza de Nueva Zelanda es una experiencia para ser disfrutada y recordada.

Page 2 & 3 Lake Alexandrina and Southern Alps in autumn.

Pagea 2 et 3: Le lac Alexandrine et les Alpes du sud en automne.

Seite 2 & 3: Alexandrinasee und Südalpen im Herbst.

Páginas 2 &3 Lago Alexandrina y Alpes del Sur en otoño.

The South Island is dominated by mountains. The Southern Alps divide west from east and create an imaginary boundary for the extremes of north and south—they separate Westland rainforest from Canterbury plains and Marlborough vineyards from Southland pastures. The mountains, many of which are over 3,000m, dictate the climate and with it South Islanders' lifestyle and livelihood. No one lives far from them, which entices climbers, skiers and tourists on alpine flights.

From the peaks run river valleys and glaciers of unsurpassed beauty, vast tussocklands, schist covered hills and lakes framed by snowclad peaks and virgin forest. Mountain passes connect the main tourist destinations of the South Island and link historic sites such as gold miners' stone cottages to pioneer sheep stations.

The scenery of the South Island is dramatic—from the entrance to the Marlborough Sounds to the fiords of Milford.

Le paysage de l'île du sud est dominé par des montagnes, les Alpes du sud, qui séparent la région ouest de la région est, créant ainsi une frontière imaginaire entre les paysages si diversifiés du nord et du sud de l'île—elles séparent les forêts tropicales de l'ouest des plaines de Canterbury, ainsi que des vignobles productifs de Marlborough et des pâturages verts du sud. Ces montagnes, dont la plupart dépassent 3 000 mètres, déterminent non seulement le climat, mais aussi le style de vie et les moyens d'existence des habitants de l'île sud.

Depuis les sommets proéminents s'étendent des vallées et des des glaciers d'une beauté extraordinaire, des prairies vastes similaires aux steppes, des monticules d'ardoises bizarres et des lacs entourés de sommets recouverts de neige et des forêts vierges.

Des chaînes de montagnes relient les destinations touristiques de l'île du sud entre elles, ainsi que les villages historiques des chercheurs d'or et des stations d'élevage de moutons fondés par les pionniers.

La diversité du paysage de l'île du sud est spectaculaire, depuis l'entrée de la région de Marlborough Sounds jusqu'aux Fjords de Milford Sound.

Die Südinsel wird landschaftlich von Bergen dominiert. Die Südalpen trennen den Westen vom Osten und schaffen ebenso eine imaginäre Grenze zwischen den so verschiedenartig gestalteten Landschaften im Norden und Süden der Insel—sie trennen die Regenwälder der Region Westland von der Canterbury Ebene und die ertragreichen Weinanbaugebiete in Marlborough von den saftigen Weiden in Southland. Die Berge, von denen viele höher als 3000 Meter sind, bestimmen das Klima und damit den Lebensstil und den Lebensunterhalt der Südinselbewohner. Niemand lebt weit von der Gebirgswelt entfernt, die Wanderer, Bergsteiger und Skifahrer begeistert und Touristen zum alpinen Rundflug verlockt.

Von den erhabenen Höhen der Bergwelt erstrekken sich Flußtäler und Gletscher von unübertroffener Schönheit, und weitläufige, steppenähnliche Graslandschaften, bizarre Schieferhügel und von schneebedeckten Gipfeln und unberührten Wäldern umgebene Seen breiten sich aus. Bergpässe verbinden die bedeutendsten touristischen Zielorte der Südinsel miteinander und stellen ebenso die Verbindung zwischen historischen Goldgräberstätten und von Pionieren gegründeten Schafstationen her.

La Isla Sur esta dominada por montañas. Los Alpes del Sur dividen el Oeste del Este y crean una frontera imaginaria desde el extremo norte al extremo sur de la isla -separan la pluviselva de Westland de las llanuras de Canterbury y los viñedos de Marlborough de las dehesas de Southland. Las montañas, muchas de las cuales superan los 3.000 metros, dictan el clima y con ello el estilo y la forma de vida de los habitantes de la Isla Sur. Desde las cimas descienden rios de valles y glaciares de insuperable belleza, vastas praderas de hierba, colinas y lagos cubiertos de esquistos enmarcados por picos revestidos de nieve y bosque virgen. Los pasos de montaña conectan los principales destinos turísticos de la Isla Sur y enlazan con emplazamientos históricos tales como las cabañas de piedra de los buscadores de oro o los ranchos de ovejas de los pioneros.

Left: The Abel Tasman National Park walkway follows the coastline through native forest and crosses golden sandy beaches. At the bottom of this photo is the Anchorage hut.

A gauche: Le sentier du parc national Abel Tasman suit le littoral à travers des forêts de la Nouvelle-Zélande et des plages de sable doré. La cabane d'Anchorage figure au premier plan.

Links: Der Wanderweg durch den Abel Tasman Nationalpark folgt dem Küstenverlauf durch heimische Waldgebiete und über goldfarbene Sandstrände. Am unteren Ende dieser Aufnahme sieht man die Anchorage Hut.

Izquierda: El sendero del Parque Nacional Abel Tasman sigue el litoral a través de bosque nativo y cruza playas de doradas arenas. Al fondo de esta foto se encuentra el albergue de Anchorage.

Left top: Picton, on Queen Charlotte Sound, has the South Island terminus for the Cook Strait ferry.

Far left: Fruit growing is important in the Nelson District as seen here in the Riwaka Valley.

Left: A strip of golden sand separates clear blue water from native bush at Te Pukatea Bay in Abel Tasman National Park.

Above: Peaceful Crail Bay in Pelorus Sound, Marlborough Sounds.

En haut à gauche: Le village de Picton, situé dans la région du Queen Charlotte Sound sur l'île sud, constitue le terminal des ferries du détroit de Cook.

A l'extrême gauche: L'arboriculture constitue une industrie importante dans la région de Nelson, comme ici la vallée de Riwaka.

A gauche: Une bande de sable doré sépare la mer bleue et claire de la forêt de la Nouvelle-Zélande de Te Pukatea Bay dans le parc national Abel Tasman.

Ci-dessus: La tranquillité de Crail Bay dans la région de Pelorus Sound, l'un des détroits pittoresques de Marlborough Sounds.

Oben links: In der Ortschaft Picton, die am Queen Charlotte Sound auf der Südinsel liegt, befindet sich der Fährhafen für die Cook Strait Fährschiffe.

Ganz links: Obstanbau stellt einen wichtigen Erwerbszweig in der Region Nelson dar, wie hier im Riwakatal.

Links: Ein Streifen goldfarbenen Strandes trennt das klare, blaue Meerwasser von der einheimischen Bewaldung der Te Pukatea Bay im Abel Tasman Nationalpark.

Oben: Die friedvolle Crail Bay im Pelorus Sound, einem der malerischen Sunde im Gebiet der Marlborough Sounds.

Superior izquierda: Picton, en Queen Charlotte Sound, cuenta con la terminal de ferry Cook Strait para la Isla Sur.

Exterior izquierda: La fruticultura es importante en la Región de Nelson tal como se puede ver aquí en el Valle de Riwaka.

Izquierda: Una franja de arena dorada separa las transparentes aguas azules del bosque nativo en Te Pukatea Bay en el Parque Nacional Abel Tasman.

Arriba: La tranquila Crail Bay en Pelorus Sound, forma parte del area conocida como Marlborough Sounds.

Far left: Whitebait are a small delicacy fish caught seasonally near river mouths throughout New Zealand, as seen here at the Aorere River bridge, Golden Bay.

Left: Verdant hills in the Upper Riwaka Valley, Nelson.

Above: The distant monument records Abel Tasman as the first European to discover New Zealand.

Ganz links: Whitebait sind kleine Fischdelikatessen, die in ganz Neuseeland saisonbedingt an den Flußmündungen gefangen werden, wie hier an der Aorerebrücke bei der Golden Bay.

Links: Grüne Hügel im Oberen Riwakatal, Nelson.

Oben: Das in der Ferne sichtbare Denkmal erinnert an Abel Tasman, den ersten Europäer, der Neuseeland im Jahre 1642 entdeckte und in die Ligar Bay einlief.

A l'extrême gauche: Les "whitebait" sont une spécialité de petits poissons que l'on pêche de façon saisonnière à l'embouchure des rivières dans toute la Nouvelle-Zélande comme ici sur le pont de la rivière Aorere à Golden Bay.

A gauche: Des collines verdoyantes dans la haute vallée de Riwakatal à Nelson.

Ci-dessus: Le monument à l'arrière-plan fut érigé en souvenir d'Abel Tasman, premier Européen à découvrir la Nouvelle-Zélande en 1642 et à poser le pied à Ligar Bay.

Exterior izquierda: Los espadines o chanquetes son un manjar de pequeños peces que se cogen estacionalmente en la desembocadura de los ríos en toda Nueva Zelanda, como se ve aquí en el puente del Río Aorere, en Golden Bay.

Izquierda: Valle de Upper Riwaka, Nelson.

Arriba: El monumento en la lejanía deja constancia de Abel Tasman como el primer europeo que descubrió Nueva Zelanda, al llegar a Ligar Bay en 1642.

Left: A pristine morning at Torrent Bay, Abel Tasman National Park.

Top: Remote Whariwiki Beach on the West Coast south of Farewell Spit.

Above: Marlborough Sounds from the air, showing the complex coastline of "drowned valleys".

Links: Prachtvolle Morgenstimmung in der Torrent Bay im Abel Tasman Nationalpark.

Oben: Der abgelegene Strand von Wharariki an der Westküste, südlich der Farewell Spit Landzunge.

Oben: Die großartige Landschaft der Marlborough Sounds aus der Vogelperspektive, die die vielfältig verflochtene Küstenlinie der 'ertränkten Täler' zeigt.

A gauche: Une matinée splendide à Torrent Bay dans le parc national Abel Tasman.

Ci-dessus: La plage isolée de Wharariki sur la côte ouest au sud de la pointe de Farewell Spit.

Ci-dessus: Une vue aérienne du paysage grandiose de Marlborough Sounds soulignant la complexité des lignes côtières entrelacées de la "vallée noyée".

Izquierda: Una prístina mañana en Torrent Bay, Parque Nacional Abel Tasman.

Superior: La remota Playa de Wharariki en West Coast (Costa Oeste) al sur de Farewell Spit.

Arriba: Panorámica aérea de Marlborough Sounds, mostrando el intrincado litoral de "valles inundados".

13

Left: The Inland Kaikoura Mountains in winter, viewed from a commercial flight between Christchurch and Wellington.

Above: Kaikoura township nestles below the Seaward Kaikoura Mountains. Boat operators take visitors to see the many whales, dolphins and seals that live close by.

A gauche: Les chaînes de montagne de Kaikoura situées vers l'intérieur du pays lors d'un vol de ligne entre Christchurch et Wellington en hiver.

Ci-dessus: La ville de Kaikoura blottie contre les montagnes de Kaikoura du côté de la mer. Les visiteurs du monde entier peuvent observer, depuis des bateaux, les baleines, les dauphins et les phoques qui passent le long des côtes.

Links: Die landeinwärts gelegene Bergkette der Kaikoura Mountains im Winter, aufgenommen während eines Linienfluges von Christchurch nach Wellington.

Oben: Die Ortschaft Kaikoura schmiegt sich an die seewärts gelegene Seite der Kaikoura Mountains an. Besucher aus aller Welt können die im Küstenbereich vorkommenden Wale, Delphine und Robben von Booten aus beobachten.

Izquierda: Las Montañas de Kaikoura del Interior en invierno, vistas desde un vuelo comercial entre Christchurch y Wellington.

Arriba: La localidad de Kaikoura se situa al abrigo de las Montañas Costeras de Kaikoura. Los touroperadores de barcos llevan a los visitantes a ver a las numerosas ballenas, delfines y focas que habitan en la zona.

Above: Lake Rotoroa in Nelson Lakes National Park is a quiet place for boating and has excellent trout fishing.

Right: The Minehaha track leads through luxuriant rain forest near Fox Glacier, South Westland.

Ci-dessus: Le lac Rotorua dans le parc national Nelson Lakes est un endroit idyllique se prêtant le mieux à la pêche aux truites.

A droite: La piste de Minehaha traverse des forêts tropicales néo-zélandaises luxuriantes non loin du Fox Glacier dans la région de South Westland.

Oben: Lake Rotoroa im Nelson Lakes Nationalpark ist ein idyllischer See, der sich bestens zum Forellenangeln eignet.

Rechts: Der Minehaha Wanderweg führt durch üppigen, neuseeländischen Regenwald nahe des Fox Gletschers in South Westland.

Arriba: Lago Rotoroa en el Parque Nacional Nelson Lakes es un apacible lugar para travesías en barca y excelente para la pesca de la trucha.

Derecha: El sendero de Minehaha conduce a través de la exuberante pluviselva cerca del Glaciar Fox en South Westland.

Above: The rugged coastline just north of the Punakaiki Pancake Rocks, on the West Coast of the South Island.

Right: The Pancake Rocks at Punakaiki, where the Tasman Sea batters the headland and at high tide often sends columns of spray into the air.

Oben: Die zerklüftete Küstenlinie etwas nördlich der Punakaiki Pancake Rocks an der Westküste der Südinsel.

Rechts: Die Pancake Rocks oder "Pfannkuchenfelsen" bei Punakaiki, auf die die Meeresgewalten der Tasmanischen See einwirken und die bei schwerer Brandung oft Gischtsäulen durch die Felsspalten in Richtung Himmel schicken.

Ci-dessus: Le littoral découpé au nord des Pancake Rocks à Punakaiki, sur la côte ouest de l'île du sud.

A droite: Les Pancake Rocks ou "Rochers en forme de galettes" de Punakaiki, sur lesquels influe la puissance de la mer de Tasmanie et qui, par temps de déferlantes, projettent souvent de l'écume par les fissure des rochers en direction des nuages.

Arriba: Abrupto litoral al norte de Punakaiki Pancakes Rocks en West Coast (Costa Oeste) en la Isla Sur.

Derecha: Pancakes Rocks ("Las Rocas Tortitas") en Punakaiki, donde el Mar de Tasmania azota el promontorio rocoso y cuando la marea sube a menudo lanza enormes columnas de agua en el aire.

Far left: A picturesque old farm building near Whataroa, Westland, with a wonderful backdrop of podocarp forest and the Southern Alps.

Left: Fox Glacier, South Westland.

Above: Lake Mapourika, South Westland, on a crystal clear morning.

Ganz links: Ein malerisches, altes Farmgebäude in der Nähe von Whataroa in der Region Westland mit neuseeländischem Podocarpaceae-Wald und den majestätischen Südalpen als herrlicher Hintergrundkulisse.

Links: Der Fox Gletscher in South Westland.

Oben: Lake Mapourika in South Westland an einem kristallklaren Morgen.

A l'extrême gauche: Un vieux bâtiment de ferme pittoresque près de Whataroa dans la région de Westland avec un arrière-plan magnifique composé d'une forêt de Podocarpaceae néo-zélandaise et des Alpes du Sud majestueuses.

A gauche: Le Fox Glacier dans le South Westland.

Ci-dessus: Le Lac Mapourika dans le South Westland par une matinée claire.

Exterior izquierda: Un pintoresco viejo granero cerca de Whataroa, en la región de Westland, con un maravilloso telón de fondo de bosque de coníferas nativo del hemisferio Sur, podo-carpa (pouskarpos), y más allá los magníficos Alpes del Sur.

Izquierda: El Glaciar Fox en South Westland.

Arriba: Lago Mapourika en South Westland en una limpia y cristalina mañana.

Far left top: Mountaineers at the head of the Fox Glacier.

Left top: Franz Josef Glacier. There are guided walks on both Fox and Franz Josef enabling visitors to venture on to the glaciers.

Left: Everyone should visit Lake Matheson and it is never more spectacular than at dawn or dusk. Sometimes the reflections are breathtaking and it is always worth the short walk.

Above: Lake Moeraki and toi tois, South Westland.

Tout en haut à gauche: Des alpinistes au sommet du Fox Glacier.

En haut à gauche: Le glacier Franz Josef. Des randonnées guidées sont organisées sur les deux glaciers, Fox et Franz Josef, ce qui permet aux touristes de s'aventurer dans cette région de glaciers fascinante.

A gauche: Vous devez absolument visiter le lac Matheson apparaissant dans toute sa splendeur à l'aube et au crépuscule. Ses reflets sont souvent stupéfiants et récompensent le visiteur après une promenade sur le lac.

Ci-dessus: Le lac Moeraki et les herbages à longues tiges Toe Toe du South Westland.

Ganz links oben: Bergsteiger im oberen Bereich des Fox Gletschers.

Links oben: Der Franz Josef Gletscher. Begleitete Gletscherwanderungen auf dem Franz Josef Glacier und Fox Glacier ermöglichen es Besuchern, sich weiter in dieses faszinierende Gletschergebiet vorzuwagen.

Links: Besuchen Sie auf jeden Fall den Lake Matheson, der sich in der Morgen- und Abenddämmerung am atemberaubendsten präsentiert. Die Reflektionen sind oft großartig und belohnen den Betrachter nach einem Spaziergang zum See.

Oben: Der Moerakisee und langstielige Toe Toe Gräser in South Westland.

Superior exterior izquierda: Montañistas en la cabeza del Glaciar Fox.

Superior izquierda: Glaciar Franz Josef. Hay excursiones organizadas que permiten a los visitantes aventurarse en ambos glaciares, Fox y Franz Josef.

Izquierda: Todo el mundo debería visitar el Lago Matheson, que nunca es más espectacular que cuando amanece y en el crepúsculo del atardecer. Algunas veces los reflejos en el lago son tan impresionantes que cortan la respiración y siempre merece la pena el corto paseo.

Arriba: Lago Moeraki y Toe-Toe (variedad nativa de altas hierbas), en South Westland.

Above: There are numerous attractive shaded walkways through the exotic pine forests around Hanmer, North Canterbury.

Top right: A tramper boils the billy in the Ada Valley on the St James walkway near the Lewis Pass.

Right: Hanmer township as viewed from the summit of Conical Hill, an easy 20 minute walk through pine forest.

Ci-dessus: Des pistes de randonnées ravissantes et ombragées dans la pinède exotique aux alentours de Hanmer Springs dans la région nord du Canterbury.

En haut à droite: Un randonneur se chauffe du fameux "billy" sur le sentier St. James dans le Adatal, près de Lewis Pass.

A droite: Une vue du village de Hanmer depuis le sommet de Conical Hill que l'on peut atteindre facilement à pied en 20 minutes à travers la pinède.

Oben: Es gibt eine Reihe reizvoller und schattiger Wanderwege durch die für Neuseeland exotischen Kiefernwälder in der Umgebung von Hanmer Springs in North Canterbury.

Oben rechts: Ein Wanderer erhitzt den sogenannten 'billy' auf dem St. James Walkway im Adatal nahe des Lewis Passes.

Rechts: Die Ortschaft Hanmer vom Gipfel des Conical Hill aus gesehen, der nach einem leichten, 20minütigen Spaziergang durch Kiefernwald erreicht werden kann.

Arriba: En la zona de Hanmer en North Canterbury existen numerosos y atractivos sombreados senderos que cruzan a través de exóticos bosques de pinos.

Superior derecha: Senderista hirviendo el cazo en el Valle de Ada, en el sendero de St. James cerca de Lewis Pass (Paso de Lewis).

Derecha: El municipio de Hanmer tal como se divisa desde la cima de Conical Hill, un sencillo paseo de 20 minutos a través de bosque de pinos.

Left: The town crier announcing events at the popular Christchurch Arts Centre's weekend market.

Above: Victoria Square, Christchurch.

Above right: The very centre of Christchurch is Cathedral Square, with its new sculpture commissioned for the millennium—Neil Dawson's *Chalice.*

Right: The azalea gardens at Ilam are open to the public. Christchurch has long been referred to as the Garden City of New Zealand.

A gauche: Le crieur publique annonce les manifestations du jour lors du marché populaire de fin de semaine au Centre des Arts à Christchurch.

Ci-dessus: Le square Victoria à Christchurch.

En haut à droite: Au centre-ville de Christchurch se trouve le Cathedral Square (Square de la cathédrale) avec ses échoppes et le célèbre "Wizard" (magicien) de midi.

A droite: Les jardins d'azalées du quartier d'Ilam sont ouverts au public. Christchurch est depuis longtemps reconnu comme la "Cité des jardins" de la Nouvelle-Zélande.

Links: Der Stadtausrufer kündigt die Veranstaltungen während des beliebten Wochenendmarktes auf dem Gelände des Christchurch Arts Centre an.

Oben links: Victoria Square in Christchurch.

Oben: Im Zentrum der Stadt Christchurch befindet sich der Cathedral Square mit seinen Marktbuden und einem be-rühmten Unterhalter zur Mittagszeit—dem Wizard.

Rechts: Die Azaleengärten von Ilam sind für jedermann zugänglich. Christchurch wird schon seit langem als "Garten-stadt Neuseelands" bezeichnet.

Izquierda: El pregonero de la ciudad anunciando el programa de actos en el popular mercadillo de los fines de semana en Christchurch Arts Centre (Centro de las Artes de Christchurch).

Arriba izquierda: Victoria Square, en Christchurch.

Arriba: En el mismo centro de Christchurch se encuen-tra Cathedral Square con sus puestos ambulantes y la actua-ción al mediodía del artista conocido como El Mago.

Derecha: Los jardines de azalea en Ilam están abiertos al público. Desde hace ya tiempo se hace alusión a Christ-church como la Ciudad de los Jardines de Nueva Zelanda.

27

Above: The road from Christchurch to the West Coast via Arthur's Pass passes this scene at Castle Hill of Highland cattle and the Torlesse Range.

Right: Governors Bay at the head of Lyttelton Harbour is only 20 minutes drive from central Christchurch.

Oben: Die Überlandstraße von Christchurch zur Westküste via Arthurs Pass führt an Castle Hill vorbei, hier mit Hochlandrindern und der Torlesse Bergkette im Hintergrund.

Rechts: Governors Bay liegt an der weiträumigen Bucht des Lyttelton Harbour und ist nur etwa 20 Autominuten vom Zentrum der Gartenstadt entfernt.

Ci-dessus: La route reliant Christchurch à la côte ouest, en passant par le col d'Arthur Pass, suit Castle Hill, avec en arrière-plan les massifs montagneux et la chaîne de montagnes Torlesse.

A droite: Governors Bay, à l'affluent du port de Lyttelton, n'est qu'à vingt minutes de route du centre de Christchurch.

Arriba: La carretera desde Christchuch a West Coast por Arthur's Pass (Paso de Arthur) cruza este escenario de ganado Highland en Castle Hill y Torlesse Range (la Cordillera Torlesse).

Derecha: Governors Bay en la entrada de Lyttelton Harbour se halla a tan sólo 20 minutos del centro de Christchurch.

Far left & left: There is lush pasture in South Canterbury on the main road to the Southern Lakes between Geraldine and Fairlie.

Above: A good crop of wool is ready to be shorn from these sheep grazing near the Canterbury foothills of the Southern Alps.

Ganz links & links: Die saftigen Weidegebiete zwischen den in South Canterbury gelegenen Orten Geraldine und Fairlie säumen die Straße zu den Southern Lakes.

Oben: Ein ansehnlicher Ertrag an Wolle wird in Kürze von diesen Schafen geschoren werden, die im Gebiet des Canterbury Vorgebirges nahe der Südalpen grasen.

A l'extrême gauche et à gauche: La région riche en pâturages entre les villages de Geraldine et de Fairlie dans la région sud de Canterbury mènent aux lacs du sud.

Ci-dessus: Le produit considérable de la tonte des moutons broutant dans le contrefort du Canterbury non loin des Alpes du sud.

Exterior izquierda & izquierda: Ricos pastizales en South Canterbury en la carretera hacia Southern Lakes entre Geraldine y Fairlie.

Arriba: Una buena cantidad de lana está lista para ser esquilada de estas ovejas pastando próximas al pie de las colinas de Canterbury en los Alpes del Sur.

Lake Tekapo is fed by glacial waters from the main divide and set in the stark tussocky landscape of the Mackenzie Basin. Visitors may enter the Church of the Good Shepherd *(above)*.

Der Tekaposee wird von Gletschern mit Wasser gespeist und ist von der kargen, von Tussockgras bedeckten Landschaft des Mackenzie Basin umgeben. Besuchern ist es gestattet, die 'Kirche des Guten Hirten' zu betreten *(oben)*.

Le lac Tekapo est alimenté par l'eau des glaciers et est entouré des paysages désolés, couverts de touffes d'herbe du bassin de MacKenzie. Les touristes peuvent entrer dans l'"Eglise du Bon Berger" *(ci-dessus)*.

El Lago Tekapo se alimenta de las aguas glaciares procedentes de la principal bifurcación y se situa en el austero paisaje de verdes extensiones de hierba en Mackenzie Basin (la Cuenca de Mackenzie) *(arriba)*.

Above: The South Island high country has a unique grandeur with its tussock covered hills and backdrop of Alps rising well over 3,000 metres.

Right: Most owners of these holiday houses beside Lake Alexandrina are keen fishermen and to protect the tranquility no power boats are allowed on the waters.

Oben: Die Hochlandgebiete der Südinsel besitzen eine ihnen eigene Erhabenheit mit ihren von Tussockgras bedeckten Hügellandschaften und der Alpenkulisse, die im Hintergrund auf über 3000 Meter ansteigt.

Rechts: Die Besitzer dieser Ferienhäuser am Alexandrinasee sind meistens auch begeisterte Angler, und um die wohltuende Stille der Umgebung zu bewahren, hat man ein Fahrverbot für Motorboote verhängt.

Ci-dessus: Les régions montagneuses de l'île du sud ont une allure grandiose et exceptionnelle avec leurs collines recouvertes de touffes d'herbe et la coulisse des Alpes qui peut s'élever jusqu'à 3 000 mètres à l'arrière-plan.

A droite: Les occupants de ces maisons de vacances sur le lac Alexandrine sont pour la plupart des fervents de pêche et, afin de préserver la tranquillité bienfaisante de ces lieux, interdisent les bateaux à moteur.

Arriba: Las tierras altas de la Isla Sur tienen una grandeza especial con sus colinas cubiertas de verde y como telón de fondo los Alpes erigiéndose bien superiores sobre los 3.000 metros de altitud.

Derecha: La mayoría de los propietarios de estas casas de vacaciones a las orillas del Lago Alexandrina son aficionados a la pesca y para preservar la paz del entorno las embarcaciones a motor están prohibidas en sus aguas.

Above: Mt Cook (left) 3,754m high and the Tasman Glacier 28km long (on the right) as seen from a scenic flight.

Right top: Mt Cook, aptly named Aorangi (the cloud piercer) by the early Maori, viewed across Lake Pukaki.

Right: Clouds over Mt Cook, which rises above the turquoise waters of Lake Pukaki, tell of an approaching westerly storm.

Ci-dessus: Le Mont Cook (à gauche) est haut de 3 754 mètres et le glacier Tasman a une longueur de 28 kilomètres (photo de droite). Vus du ciel, ces deux endroits émerveillent le visiteur.

En haut à droite: Le Mont Cook depuis le lac Pukaki, surnommé Aorangi (force qui pénètre les nuages) par les premiers Maoris.

A droite: Les nuages au-dessus du Mont Cook, que l'eau turquoise du lac Pukaki reflète de façon majestueuse, annoncent le mauvais temps venant de l'ouest.

Oben: Der Mount Cook (links) ist 3754 Meter hoch, der Tasman Gletscher ist 28 km lang (auf der rechten Bildseite), und beide kann man bei einem Rundflug bewundern.

Oben rechts: Mount Cook, von den frühen Maoris bezeichnenderweise auch Aorangi (Durchstecher der Wolken) genannt, vom Pukakisee aus gesehen.

Rechts: Die Wolken über dem Mount Cook, der majestätisch über dem türkisfarbenen Wasser des Lake Pukaki aufragt, kündigen einen aus Westen kommenden Sturm an.

Arriba: Mt Cook (izquierda) 3.754 metros de altitud y el Glaciar Tasman 28Kms de largo (a la derecha) vistos desde un vuelo escénico.

Superior derecha: Mt Cook, acertadamente llamado por los primeros Maories Aorangi ("el perforador de nubes"), visto desde el otro lado del Lago Pukaki.

Derecha: Nubes sobre Mt Cook, que se erige sobre las aguas turquesas del Lago Pukaki, anuncian la proximidad de una tormenta por el oeste.

Far left: Mt Earnslaw at the head of Lake Wakatipu.

Left: Two skifields service Queenstown. The Remarkables pictured here and Coronet Peak.

Above: An autumn scene near Queenstown in Central Otago.

Ganz links: Mount Earnslaw am Beginn des Wakatipusees.

Links: Zwei Skigebiete bieten Queenstown Wintersport-möglichkeiten. Das hier gezeigte Remarkables Skigebiet und Coronet Peak.

Oben: Eine Herbstszene nahe bei Queenstown in Central Otago.

A l'extrême gauche: Le Mont Earnshaw à l'extrémité du lac Wakatipu.

A gauche: Deux stations de ski offre à Queenstown des activités d'hiver. Ci-contre les pistes de ski Remarkables et Coronet Peak.

Ci-dessus: Une scène d'automne près de Queenstown dans la région de Central Otago.

Exterior izquierda: Mt Earnslaw en la cabecera del Lago Wakatipu.

Izquierda: Dos estaciones de esquí sirven a la turística ciudad de Queenstown. La estación de The Remarkables que se muestra en la fotografía y Coronet Peak.

Arriba: Paisaje otoñal cerca de Queenstown en Central Otago.

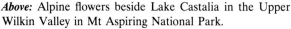

Above: Alpine flowers beside Lake Castalia in the Upper Wilkin Valley in Mt Aspiring National Park.

Above right: A winter view of Fiordland National Park seen from the scenic flight between Queenstown and Milford Sound.

Right: The summit of the Remarkables Range from Queenstown.

Ci-dessus: Des plantes alpestres près du lac Castalia dans la vallée supérieure de Wilkintal, dans le parc national du Mont Aspiring.

En haut à droite: Une vue aérienne hivernale du parc national de Fiordland lors d'un vol entre Queenstown et Milford Sound.

A droite: Le sommet de la chaîne des montagnes Remarkables à Queenstown.

Oben links: Alpenblumen beim Castaliasee im Oberen Wilkintal, Mount Aspiring Nationalpark.

Oben: Eine winterliche Ansicht des Fiordland National-parks auf einem Panoramaflug von Queenstown zum Milford Sound.

Rechts: Die Gipfel der Remarkables Bergkette von Queens-town aus gesehen.

Arriba Izquierda: Flores alpinas al pie del Lago Castalia en el Valle Upper Wilkin en el Parque Nacional Mt Aspiring.

Arriba: Panorámica invernal del Parque Nacional Fiorland visto desde un vuelo escénico entre Queenstown y Milford Sound.

Derecha: La cima de la cordillera de The Remarkables contemplada desde Queenstown.

Top: Jet boating on the Shotover River below the Edith Cavell bridge.

Above: Tranquil Glendhu Bay, Lake Wanaka.

Right: Queenstown, Lake Wakatipu and the Remarkables Range viewed from the Skyline Gondola station.

Oben: Jetbootfahrt auf dem Shotoverfluß unterhalb der Edith Cavell Brücke.

Oben: Die.stille Glendhu Bay, Lake Wanaka.

Rechts: Queenstown, der Wakatipusee und die Remarkables Bergkette von der Skyline Seilbahnstation aus gesehen.

En haut: Un tour en bateau à réaction sur la rivière Shotover, sous le pont Edith Cavell.

Ci-dessus: La baie tranquille de Glendu sur le lac Wanaka.

A droite: Queenstown, le lac Wakatipu et la chaîne de montagnes Remarkables depuis la station des gondole Skyline.

Superior: Lancha de motor a propulsión sobre el Rio Shotover bajo el Puente de Edith Cavell.

Arriba: La tranquila Glendhu Bay, Lago Wanaka.

Derecha: Queenstown, Lago Wakatipu y la cordillera de The Remarkables vistas desde la estación de góndola Skyline.

Left top: The Darren Mountains from the Key Summit tarns on the Routeburn Track.

Far left: Native Beech forest in the Eglinton Valley on the road between Te Anau and Milford.

Left: Trampers rest on a remote track in Aspiring National Park.

Above: Sutherland Falls viewed from the Milford Track, Fiordland National Park.

En haut à gauche: Les montagnes Darren depuis un lac au sommet de Key sur le sentier de Routeburn.

A l'extrême gauche: Une hêtraie de Nouvelle-Zélande dans la vallée d'Eglintontal sur le chemin de Te Anau après Milford.

A gauche: Des randonneurs se reposent sur une piste isolée dans le parc national du Mont Aspiring.

Ci-dessus: Les chutes Sutherland du Milford Track dans le parc national Fiordland.

Oben links: Der Blick auf die Darren Mountains von den Bergseen des Key Summit, Routeburn Track.

Ganz links: Neuseeländischer Südbuchenwald im Eglintontal auf dem Weg von Te Anau nach Milford.

Links: Wanderer legen eine Ruhepause auf einem entlegenen Wanderweg im Mount Aspiring Nationalpark ein.

Oben: Die Sutherland Falls im Fiordland Nationalpark, vom Milford Track aus gesehen.

Superior izquierda: Las Montañas Darren desde las lagunas Key Summit en el Sendero de Routeburn (Routeburn Track).

Exterior Izquierda: Bosque nativo de haya en el Valle Eglinton en la carretera entre Te Anau y Milford.

Izquierda: Senderistas descansan en un apartado camino en el Parque Nacional de Aspiring.

Arriba: Las Cataratas Sutherland (Sutherland Falls) en el Parque Nacional Fiorland vistas desde el Sendero de Milford.

Left: Lake Te Anau and the Murchison Mountains.

Above: The road from Te Anau to Milford Sound through the Upper Hollyford Valley is one of the world's finest drives. Coach windows provide continuous magnificent sights such as this one at Falls Creek.

Links: Lake Te Anau und die Murchison Berge.

Oben: Die Straße, die von der Ortschaft Te Anau durch das Obere Hollyfordtal zum Milford Sound führt, gehört zu einer der landschaftlich schönsten Fahrten der Welt. Die ununterbrochenen, großartigen Anblicke können durch die Fenster der Reisebusse genossen werden, wie hier beim Falls Creek.

A gauche: Le lac Te Anau et les montagnes Murchison.

Ci-dessus: La route partant du village de Te Anau et conduisant à Milford Sound en passant par la vallée supérieure de Hollyfordtal, est considéré comme l'un des plus beaux paysages du monde. Vous pouvez observer, à travers les fenêtres de l'autocar, des vues splendides et continuelles, comme celle-ci prise à Falls Creek.

Izquierda: Lago Te Anau y las Montañas de Murchison.

Arriba: La carretera desde Te Anau a Milford Sound a través del Valle Upper Hollyford es uno de los trayectos más hermosos del mundo. Las ventanas de los autocares proveen al visitante continuamente con magníficas vistas tales como ésta de las Cascadas Creek.

Previous page: Mitre Peak and Milford Sound.

Left top: Delightful old buildings in Stuart Street, Dunedin.

Left: Victorian architecture of Dunedin Railway Station.

Above: Sited at the head of Otago Harbour is Dunedin with its centre in the shape of an octagon.

Page précédente: Mitre Peak et Milford Sound.

En haut à gauche: De vieux immeubles charmants dans la rue Stuart à Dunedin.

A gauche: L'architecture victorienne de la gare de Dunedin.

Ci-dessus: A l'extrémité du port d'Otago se situe Dunedin, avec son centre-ville en forme d'octogone.

Vorhergehende Seite: Mitre Peak und Milford Sound.

Oben links: Reizvolle, altehrwürdige Gebäude in der Stuart Street, Dunedin.

Links: Viktorianische Architektur des Hauptbahnhofs von Dunedin.

Oben: Am Anfang der Otago Hafenbucht liegt die Stadt Dunedin mit ihrem achteckigen Stadtzentrum, dem Octagon.

Página anterior: El Pico Mitre y Milford Sound.

Superior izquierda: Precioso edificio antiguo en Stuart Street, Dunedin.

Izquierda: La arquitectura victoriana de la Estación de Ferrocarril de Dunedin.

Arriba: Situado en la cabecera de Otago Harbour está Dunedin con su centro urbano en forma de octágono.

Above: Moeraki Boulders are a geological curiosity 2km south of Hampden on the South Island's east coast.

Right: Bluff Harbour and the Aluminium Smelter at Tiwai Point, Southland.

Far right: A tranquil lookout over Patterson Inlet, Stewart Island.

Oben: Die Moeraki Steinkugeln stellen eine geologische Kuriosität dar und sind etwa zwei Kilometer südlich von Hampden an der Ostküste der Südinsel vorzufinden.

Rechts: Der Hafen von Bluff und die Aluminiumschmelzerei am Tiwai Point, Southland.

Ganz rechts: Der friedvolle Anblick des Patterson Meeresarmes auf der Stewart Insel.

Ci-dessus: Les Moeraki Boulders sont une curiosité géologique à 2 kilomètres au sud d'Hampden sur la côte est de l'île du sud.

A droite: Le port de Bluff et la fonderie d'aluminium à Tiwai Point (Southland).

Ci-contre: Une vue paisible de l'anse de Patterson sur l'île Stewart.

Arriba: Los Cantos de Moeraki (Moeraki Boulders) constituyen una curiosidad geológica 2 Kms al sur de Hampden en la costa este de la Isla Sur.

Derecha: Bluff Harbour y el Horno de Fundición de Aluminio en Tiwai Point, Southland.

Exterior Derecha: Tranquilo atalaya sobre Patterson Inlet, Stewart Island.

If New Zealand's landscape is diverse, so too is its climate. The far north boasts a sub-tropical climate, with mile upon mile of golden sandy beaches shaded by giant pohutukawas. The quality of deep sea fishing in the Bay of Islands is recognised worldwide and though few stands remain, Northland's kauri forests speak of a majestic past. In the Central Plateau is a geothermal area, with spectacular geysers, boiling mud pools and on Mt Ruapehu, a steaming crater lake, surrounded by snowclad volcanic peaks.

Another feature of the North Island is the larger Maori population with its tradition and history, especially in remote coastal areas, where life still evolves with and around the land, the sea and the marae. The North Island has much to offer the visitor geographically, culturally and historically.

Wenn Neuseelands Landschaften sich schon so verschiedenartig präsentieren, dann kann das gleiche auch von dem hier herrschenden Klima behauptet werden. Im Hohen Norden findet man subtropisches Klima und kilometerlange, goldfarbene Sandstrände vor, deren kühlender Schatten von gigantischen Pohutukawa-Bäumen gespendet wird. Das Hochseeangeln im Gebiet der Bay of Islands ist weltberühmt, und die noch überlebenden Kauriwälder der Region Northland zeugen von der majestätischen Vergangenheit dieser Baumriesen in diesem Land. Das zentrale Hochplateau ist ein geothermisches Gebiet mit spektakulären Geysiren, brodelnden Schlammtümpeln und einem dampfenden Kratersee im Gebiet des Mount Ruapehu Vulkans.

Die Nordinsel hat einen gegenüber der Südinsel weitaus größeren Bevölkerungsanteil an Maoris mit ihrer eigenständigen Tradition und Geschichte vorzuweisen, und zwar besonders in entlegenen Küstengebieten, in denen ihre Lebensart noch vom Land, dem Ozean und dem Marae, dem Versammlungshaus der Maoris, bestimmt wird. Die Nordinsel kann ihren Besuchern viele interessante geographische, kulturelle und geschichtliche Besonderheiten bieten.

Les paysages de la Nouvelle-Zélande sont très variés. L'extrême nord est caractérisé par des plages de sable doré ombragées par de gigantesques Pohutukawa et les vestiges de la forêt de kauris attestent d'un passé majestueux.

La pêche hauturière dans la région de Bay of Islands est renommée à travers le monde, ainsi que la région géothermique du Plateau central avec ses volcans, ses geysers spectaculaires et ses bassins de boue bouillante.

L'île du nord se caractérise également par l'importance de sa population Maori, particulièrement dans des régions peu peuplées où leur mode de vie gravite encore autour de la terre, de la mer et du "Marae", lieu de réunion des Maoris. L'île du nord offre aux tourists un grand nombre d'attractions, qu'elles soient géographiques, culturelles ou historiques.

El paisaje de Neuva Zelanda es diverso. El extremo norte está formado por playas doradas sombreadas por gigantescos pohutukawas y por los vestigios aún existentes de bosques de Kauri que hablan de un pasado majestuoso. La pesca de gran altura en Bay of Islands es mundialmente reconocida como lo es asimismo la actividad geotermal de la Meseta Central, con sus cimas volcánicas, espectaculares geiseres y charcas de barro hirviente.

La Isla Norte tiene un población maorí más extensa, especialmente en areas remotas, donde la vida todavía se desenvuelve en torno a la tierra, el mar y el marae. La Isla Norte tiene mucho que ofrecer geograficamente, culturalmente e historicamente.

Left: Cape Reinga at the North of New Zealand is of special significance in Maori folklore. Departed spirits leave for their homeland from a pohutukawa tree clinging to this rock.

A gauche: Le cap Reinga à la pointe nord de la Nouvelle-Zélande a une signification particulière pour les Maoris. En effet l'âme de leurs ancêtres effectue le voyage vers le paradis depuis un arbre Pohutukawa qui s'est accroché à ce rocher.

Links: Cape Reinga an der Nordspitze Neuseelands hat eine besondere Bedeutung für die Maoris. Die Seelen ihrer Verstorbenen treten ihre Reise ins Ursprungsland von einem Pohutukawa-Baum an, der sich an diesen Felsen klammert.

Izquierda: Cape Reinga en el norte de Nueva Zelanda tiene una especial relevancia en el folklore Maorí. Espíritus difuntos parten para su tierra natal desde el árbol del pohutukawa que se aferra a esta roca.

Left top: The cruise boat *Tiger III* at Piercy Rock, Cape Brett, the entrance to the Bay of Islands.

Above left: The Rainbow Falls near Keri Keri, Bay of Islands.

Left: Pleasure yachts moored in Matauwhi Bay, Bay of Islands.

Above: This giant kauri in Waipoua Forest is known as Tane Mahuta (Lord of the Forest). It is 51m high, 14m around and is believed to be 1,200 years old.

A l'extrême gauche: Le yacht de croisière, Tiger III, à Piercy Rock au cap Brett à l'entrée de Bay of Islands.

En haut à gauche: Les chutes Rainbow près de Kerikeri, Bay of Islands.

A gauche: Des yachts amarrés dans la baie de Matauwhi, Bay of Islands.

Ci-dessus: Cet énorme arbre Kauri dans la forêt de Waipoua est connu sous le nom de Tane Mahuta (Roi de la forêt). Il mesure 51 mètres de hauteur et 14 mètres de circonférence. Il est âgé de 1 200 ans.

Oben links: Das Ausflugsboot Tiger III beim Piercy Rock am Kap Brett, der Einfahrt zur Bay of Islands, der bekaunten Bucht der Inseln.

Oben links: Die Rainbow Falls nahe Kerikeri, Bay of Islands.

Links: Vertäute Jachten in Matauwhi Bay, Bay of Islands.

Oben: Dieser gigantische Kauribaum im Waipouawald trägt den Namen Tane Mahuta (Gebieter des Waldes). Er ist 51 Meter hoch, hat einen Umfang von 14 Metern und ein geschätztes Alter von etwa 1200 Jahren.

Superior izquierda: El yate-crucero Tiger III en Piercy Rock, Cabo Brett, a la entrada de Bay of Islands.

Arriba izquierda: Las Cataratas Rainbow (Rainbow Falls) cerca de Keri Keri, Bay of Islands.

Izquierda: Embarcaciones de recreo atracadas en Matauwhi Bay, Bay of Islands.

Arriba: Este colosal Kauri en el Bosque de Waipoua es conocido como Tane Mahuta (El Señor del Bosque). Mide 51 metros de altitud, 14 metros de circunferencia y se cree que tiene 1.200 años

Left top: Tourist buses on daily trips to Cape Reinga, drive on the sands of 90 mile Beach.

Left: Opito Bay anchorage, Bay of Islands.

Above: Sunbathers from the Department of Conservation campsite at Matai Bay, Northland, shelter behind a pohutukawa clad headland.

Ci-dessus: Des cars passent par la plage de sable de Ninety Mile Beach pour effectuer leur excursion quotidienne au Cap Reinga.

Ci-contre: L'ancrage dans la baie d'Opito, Bay of Islands.

En haut à droite: Des personnes du camping du Département pour la Protection de l'Environnement dans la baie de Matai, Northland, prennent un bain de soleil sous les arbres Pohutakawa.

Oben links: Reisebusse befahren den Sandstrand des Ninety Mile Beach auf ihrem täglichen Ausflug zum Kap Reinga.

Links: Ankerplatz in der Bucht von Opito, Bay of Islands.

Oben: Sonnenbadende vom Department of Conservation Campingplatz in der Matai Bay, Northland, genießen eine geschützte Stelle der von Pohutukawa-Bäumen gesäumten Bucht.

Superior izquierda: Autocares turísticos en excursiones diarias al Cabo Reinga, conducen a través de la arena en la Playa de las 90 Millas.

Izquierda: Embarcadero de Opito Bay, Bay of Islands.

Arriba: Bañistas del cámping del Departamento de Conservación de Recursos Naturales en Matai Bay, al resguardo de un promontorio rocoso revestido de Pohutukawas.

Left top: Shelter belts create a micro-climate for the extensive citrus orchards at Kerikeri.

Left: Modern craft moor in Kerikeri Basin in front of New Zealand's oldest stone store and surviving residence.

Above: Otehei Bay, Urupukapuka Island, the site of Zane Grey's camp, is today part of the Bay of Islands Maritime Park.

En haut à gauche: Les régions abritées de Kerikeri produisent un microclimat propice aux vastes vergers d'agrumes.

A gauche: Des embarcations modernes amarrées dans le bassin de Kerikeri en face du dock le plus vieux de la Nouvelle-Zélande.

Ci-dessus: La baie d'Otehei sur l'île Urupukapukam, autrefois camp du fameux écrivain Zane Grey, fait maintenant partie du parc maritime de Bay of Islands.

Oben links: Schützende Baumgürtel schaffen ein Mikroklima für die ausgedehnten Zitrusfrucht-Anbaugebiete in Kerikeri.

Links: Moderne Boote sind im Kerikeri Becken vor Neuseelands ältestem Lagerhaus aus Stein und dem ältesten, noch bestehenden Wohngebäude vertäut.

Oben: Die Bucht von Otehei auf der Urupukapuka Insel war einmal der Lagerplatz des berühmten Schriftstellers Zane Grey und ist heute Teil des Bay of Islands Maritime Park.

Superior izquierda: Las franjas de protección árbolea crean un micro-clima para las extensas huertas de cultivos de cítricos en Keri keri.

Izquierda: Modernas embarcaciones atracadas en Kerikeri Basin delante del almacén de piedra y la residencia más antiguas de Nueva Zelanda que aún hoy día perduran.

Arriba: Otehei Bay, en la Isla Urupukapuka, es el enclave del campamento de Zane Grey, que forma parte en la actualidad del Parque Marítimo de Bay of Islands

Left: The Georgian Treaty House at Waitangi, where in 1840 Maori chiefs signed the historic document with representatives of British Sovereignty.

Above left: Paihia is an important tourist centre and starting point for boat trips to the Bay of Islands Maritime Park.

Above: Peaceful Russell was once a whaling port called Kororareka, with a reputation as the "hell-hole of the Pacific".

A gauche: La résidence de James Busby à Waitangi, connue sous le nom de Maison du Traîté, où les chefs de plusieurs tribus Maoris ont, en 1840, signé le Traîté historique de Waitangi avec des représentants de la Couronne britannique.

En haut à gauche: Paihia est non seulement un endroit touristique prépondérant, mais aussi le point de départ des bateaux d'excursion allant vers le parc maritime de Bay of Islands.

En haut à droite: Russell, un village aujourd'hui paisible, fut autrefois un port de pêche à la baleine avec le nom de Kororareka qui, à cette époque, avait la réputation d'être "l'enfer du Pacifique."

Links: Die als Treaty House bekannte Residenz von James Busby in Waitangi, auf deren Gelände die Häuptlinge mehrerer Maoristämme im Jahre 1840 den historischen Vertrag von Waitangi mit Vertretern der Britischen Krone abschlossen.

Oben links: Paihia ist ein bedeutendes touristisches Zentrum und der Ausgangspunkt für Bootsausflüge in den Bay of Islands Maritime Park.

Oben: Der heute friedvolle Ort Russell war früher einmal ein Hafenort für Walfänger mit Namen Kororareka, der damals mit dem Namen "Höllenloch des Pazifiks" belegt wurde.

Izquierda: El edificio de estilo georgiano de la Casa de Tratados (Treaty House) en Waitangi, donde en 1840 los jefes maories firmaron el documento histórico conocido como el Tratado de Waitangi con los representantes de la Corona Británica.

Arriba izquierda: Paihia es un importante centro turístico y el punto de partida para las excursiones en barco que salen hacia el Parque Marítimo Bay of Islands.

Arriba: La tranquila localidad de Russell que en otros tiempos fue un puerto ballenero conocido como Kororareka, con reputación de ser "el infierno del Pacífico".

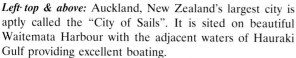

Left-top & above: Auckland, New Zealand's largest city is aptly called the "City of Sails". It is sited on beautiful Waitemata Harbour with the adjacent waters of Hauraki Gulf providing excellent boating.

Left: On the west coast of Auckland is the surfing beach of Piha.

Above right: A haven in central Auckland is Albert Park, overlooked by the University clocktower.

Ci-dessus à gauche et ci-dessus: Auckland, la plus grande ville de la Nouvelle-Zélande, est reconnue à bon droit comme étant la "Ville des voiliers." Auckland est située à l'extrémité du port de Waitemata, en face du golfe Hauraki, constituant ainsi un endroit idéal pour la voile.

A gauche: Piha, une plage de surf située sur la côte ouest d'Auckland.

En haut à droite: Le Parc Albert, un havre de paix, au coeur d'Auckland ; il est surplombé par l'horloge de l'université.

Oben links & oben: Auckland, die größte Stadt Neuseelands, wird mit Recht auch als "Stadt der Segel" bezeichnet. Auckland liegt an der prächtigen Hafenbucht des Waitemata Harbour, und die benachbarten Gewässer des Hauraki Gulf eignen sich hervorragend zum Segeln.

Links: An der Westküste Aucklands liegt der Strand von Piha, der zum Wellenreiten einlädt.

Oben rechts: Albert Park ist eine beliebte Grünanlage im Herzen von Auckland und wird von der Turmuhr der Universität überragt.

Izquierda superior & arriba: Auckland, la ciudad más grande de Nueva Zelanda es acertadamente llamada "La Ciudad de las Velas".Está situada en el hermoso Waitemata Harbour con las adyacentes aguas del Golfo de Hauraki que favorecen una magnífica navegación.

Izquierda: En la costa oeste de Auckland se halla la Playa de Piha extraordinaria para practicar el surf.

Arriba derecha: Un refugio en el centro de Auckland es Albert Park, visto desde la torre del reloj de la Universidad.

Left: Surfers at Ocean Beach, Mt Maunganui.

Above: The boat harbour of Tauranga with Mt Maunganui in the distance.

Right: Hamilton, New Zealand's largest inland city is beautifully situated on the Waikato River and services a rich farming area.

Links: Wellenreiter am Ocean Beach, Mount Maunganui.

Oben: Der Bootshafen von Tauranga mit Mount Maunganui im Hintergrund.

Rechts: Hamilton, Neuseelands größte inländische Stadt, säumt den Waikatofluß und betreut ein weiträumiges und sehr ertragreiches landwirtschaftliches Gebiet.

A gauche: Des surfeurs à Ocean Beach, Mont Maunganui.

Ci-dessus: Le port de Tauranga avec le Mont Maunganui à l'arrière-plan.

A droite: Hamilton, la plus grande ville intérieure de la Nouvelle-Zélande. Elle borde la rivière Waikato et entretient une région agricole étendue et très productive.

Izquierda: Surferos en Ocean Beach, Mt Maunganui.

Arriba: El puerto pesquero de Tauranga con el Monte Maunganui en la distancia.

Derecha: Hamilton, la ciudad del interior más grande de Nueva Zelanda está maravillosamente situada en el Rio Waikato y provee con servicios a una extensa area de ricas y productivas granjas.

Above: Te Ororoa Point on the east coast of Coromandel Peninsula, just north of Pauanui.

Right top: Whitianga on the east coast of the Coromandel is a favourite holiday destination.

Right: Port Jackson at the north western extremity of Coromandel Peninsula.

Ci-dessus: Te Ororoa Point sur la côte est de la péninsule Coromandel, au nord de Pauanui.

En haut à droite: Whitianga sur la côte est de Coromandel est la destination préférée des touristes.

A droite: Port Jackson à l'extrémité nord-ouest de la péninsule Coromandel.

Oben: Te Ororoa Point an der Ostküste der Coromandel-Halbinsel, etwas nördlich von Pauanui gelegen.

Oben rechts: Whitianga, im östlichen Küstengebiet von Coromandel gelegen, ist ein beliebter Ferienort.

Rechts: Port Jackson am nordwestlichen Ende der Coromandel-Halbinsel.

Arriba: Te Ororoa Point en la costa este de la Península de Coromandel justamente al norte de Pauanui.

Superior derecha: Whitianga en la costa este de Coromandel es un destino de vacaciones muy popular.

Derecha: Port Jackson en el extremo occidental norte de la Península de Coromandel.

Left: Tree ferns beside the road at Pohuehue, Northland.

Above: A tranquil evening at tidal Whangapoua Harbour, Coromandel Peninsula.

Right: A dairy farm below the Coromandel Range near Whangapoua.

Links: Baumfarne säumen die Straße bei Pohuehue in Northland.

Oben: Besinnliche Abendstimmung beim Whangapoua Harbour, Coromandel-Halbinsel.

Rechts: Eine Milchfarm in der Nähe von Whangapoua, am Fuße der Coromandel Bergkette.

A gauche: Des fougères parsèment la route de Pohuhue, Northland.

Ci-dessus: Une soirée d'été tranquille au port Whangapoua, dans la péninsule Coromandel.

A droite: Une laiterie située dans les environs de Whangapoua, au pied de la chaîne de Coromandel.

Izquierda: Arboles de helechos al lado de la carretera en Pohuehue, Northland.

Arriba: Un tranquilo atardecer con la bajamar en Whangapoua Harbour, Península de Coromandel.

Derecha: Una vaquería al pie de la Sierra de Coromandel (Coromadel Range) cerca de Whangapoua.

Left: Waikato farmland with a horse training track in the foreground.

Above: White Island, a volcanic mountain rising out of the Bay of Plenty, is the scene of continuous and often fierce thermal activity.

Right: Blandford Lodge Stud Farm near Matamata is one of many in the Waikato.

A gauche: Des pâturages dans la région de Waikato avec une piste de dressage pour les chevaux de course au premier plan.

Ci-dessus: White Island est une montagne volcanique dans la région de Bay of Plenty qui est fréquemment en activité géothermique.

A droite: Blanford Lodge Stud Farm près de Matamata est l'un des nombreux haras de la région de Waikato.

Links: Weideland im Waikatogebiet mit einer Pferderenn-bahn im Vordergrund.

Oben: Die aus dem Wasser der Bay of Plenty emporragende White Island Vulkaninsel ist der Schauplatz ununterbroche-ner und oft heftiger geothermischer Aktivität.

Rechts: Das Blandford Lodge Gestüt nahe Matamata ist eines von vielen im Waikatogebiet.

Izquierda: Tierras de labranza en Waikato con pista ecuestre en un primer plano.

Arriba: White Island, una montaña volcánica que se erige en Bay of Plenty, es el escenario de continua y frecuente actividad termal.

Derecha: La Granja de Sementales Brandford Lodge cerca de Matamata es una de las muchas en la zona de Waikato.

Apart from the holidaymakers in mid summer, the eastern Bay of Plenty is quiet with good beaches and fishing, as here at Whanarua Bay (*Left*) and Lottin Point (*Above*).

L'été mise à part, la côte est de Bay of Plenty est une région tranquille avec des plages très agréables et offrant des points de pêche cotés, comme Whanarua *(à gauche)* et Lottin Point *(ci-dessus)*.

Von der Urlaubssaison im Hochsommer abgesehen, ist die östliche Bay of Plenty sonst eine eher beschauliche Gegend, die schöne Strände und ausgezeichnete Angelplätze bietet, wie hier die Whanarua Bay *(links)* und Lottin Point *(oben)*.

Aparte de los turistas de mediados de verano, la zona este de Bay of Plenty es tranquila con buenas playas y buena pesca, como aquí en Whanarua Bay *(Izquierda)* y Lottin Point *(Arriba)*.

Top: A dairy farm at Tapapa near Rotorua with the Kaimai Range behind.

Above: Simple holiday houses on beautiful remote Waihau Beach, East Coast.

Right: The unspoiled coast at Hicks Bay, East Cape.

Ganz oben: Eine Milchfarm bei Tapapa in der Nähe von Rotorua mit der Kaimai Bergkette im Hintergrund.

Oben: Schlichte Ferienhäuser am wunderschönen, entlegenen Waihau Beach an der Ostküste der Nordinsel.

Rechts: Die unberührte Küstengegend der Hicks Bay am East Cape.

En haut: Une laiterie à Tapapa près de Rotorua avec la chaîne de montagnes Kaimai à l'arrière-plan.

Ci-dessus: Des petites maisons de vacances sur la superbe plage isolée de Waihau sur la côte est de l'île nord.

A droite: Le littoral vierge de Hicks Bay (East Cape).

Superior: Granja de vacas en Tapapa cerca de Rotorua con la Cordillera Kaimai detrás.

Arriba: Sencillas casitas de vacaciones en la hermosa y aislada Playa de Waihau, East Coast (Costa Este).

Derecha: La costa en su estado natural en Hicks Bay, East Cape.

Left top: Taupo's boat marina at sunset with Mt Ngauruhoe in the distance.

Far left: Mt Ngauruhoe, 2,291m, is an active volcano in Tongariro National Park.

Left: The mountains of Tongariro National Park as seen from Lake Taupo.

Above: Mt Ruapehu, 2,797m, with its crater lake, photographed in mid winter.

En haut à gauche: La Marina de Taupo sous un coucher de soleil avec le Mont Ngauruhoe à l'arrière-plan.

A l'extrême gauche: Le Mont Ngauruhoe, d'une hauteur de 2 291 mètres, est un volcan en activité situé dans le parc national de Tongariro.

A gauche: Les montagnes du volcan dans le parc national de Tongariro depuis le lac Taupo.

Ci-dessus: Le Mont Ruapehu, d'une hauteur de 2 797 mètres, avec son lac de cratère en plein hiver.

Oben links: Taupos Bootsanlegeplätze bei Sonnenuntergang mit dem Mount Ngauruhoe Vulkan in der Ferne.

Ganz links: Der Mount Ngauruhoe, 2291 Meter hoch, ist ein aktiver Vulkan im Tongariro Nationalpark.

Links: Die Vulkanberge des Tongariro Nationalparks vom Tauposee aus gesehen.

Oben: Mount Ruapehu, 2797 Meter hoch, mit seinem Kratersee, im Mittwinter aufgenommen.

Superior izquierda: El puerto deportivo de Taupo al atardecer con Mt Ngauruhoe en la distancia.

Exterior izquierda: Mt Ngauruhoe, 2.291m, es un volcán activo en el Parque Nacional Tongariro.

Izquierda: Las montañas del Parque Nacional de Tongariro vistas desde el Lago Taupo.

Arriba: Mt Ruapehu, 2.797 m, con su lago en el cráter, fotografiado a mediados de invierno.

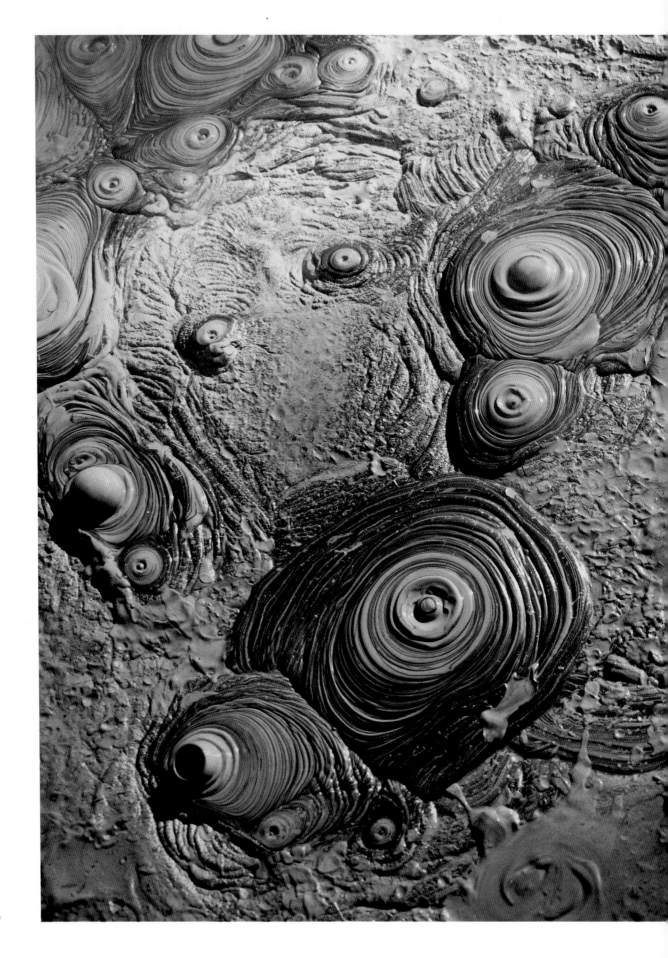

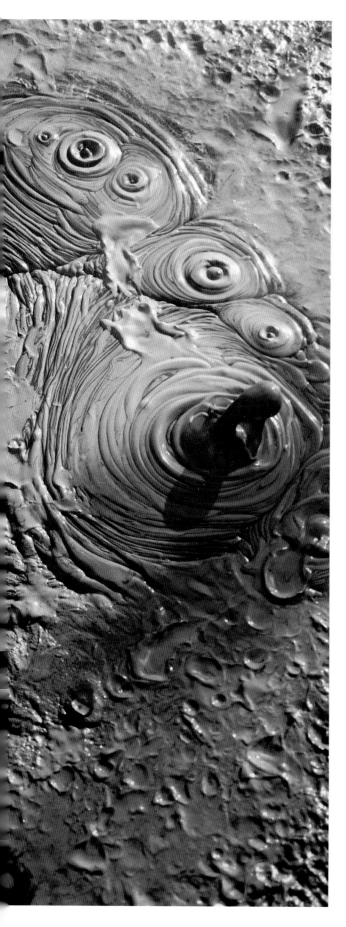

Rotorua and surrounding districts offer excellent chances to view geothermal activity. This is the boiling mud at Waimungu *(Left)* and Pohutu Geyser, Whakarewarewa.

Rotorua und Umgebung bieten ausgezeichnete Möglichkeiten, die geothermische Aktivität dieser Gegend zu erleben. Brodelnder Schlamm in Waimangu *(links)* und der Pohutu Geysir in Whakarewarewa.

La région de Rotorua offre de merveilleuses opportunités de découvrir l'activité géothermique de cette région. Mares de boue bouillantes à Waimungu *(à gauche)* et geyser Pohutu à Whakarewarewa.

Rotorua y las zonas de los alrededores ofrecen excelentes oportunidades para ver actividad geotérmica. Este es el barro hirviente en Waimungu *(Izquierda)* y el Géiser Pohutu, Whakarewarewa.

Left top: Layers of silaceous material have built up the Warbrick Terraces at Waimungu Thermal Valley.

Left bottom: Rainbow Springs trout pool, Rotorua.

Left: The Mt Tarawera volcanic rent was created in 1886 when the mountain exploded and split in two.

Oben links: Vielfältige Silikatschichten haben die Warbrick Terraces im Waimangu Thermaltal geschaffen.

Unten links: Ein Forellenteich im Rainbow Springs Park in Rotorua.

Links: Der längliche Vulkankrater des Mount Tarawera entstand im Jahre 1886, als eine gewaltige Explosion den Berg in zwei Hälften spaltete.

En haut à gauche: De nombreuses couches de silicat ont formé les terraces de Warbrick dans la vallée thermale de Waimungu.

En bas à gauche: Un plan d'eau plein de truites au parc de Rainbow Springs (Rotorua).

A gauche: Le cratère volcanique allongé du Mont Tarawera s'est formé en 1886 lors d'une puissante explosion qui a fracturé la montagne en deux parties.

Superior izquierda: Estratos de material silicoso se han ido formando en Warbrick Terraces en el Valle Termal de Waimungu.

Inferior izquierda: Las charcas de truchas de Rainbow Springs, Rotorua.

Izquierda: La hendedura volcánica de Mt Tarawera se originó en 1886 cuando la montaña explotó y se dividió en dos.

Above: A traditional entrance to a Maori meeting house at Te Kuiti, Waikato.

Right: Maori women entertainers with a poi dance at Whakarewarewa Village, Rotorua.

Above right: Young Maori warriors perform a haka (dance) at the Waitangi Treaty celebrations.

Ci-dessus: L'entrée traditionelle d'un "Marae", lieu de réunion Maori à Te Kuiti (Waikato).

Ci-dessus à droite: L'interprétation d'une dance "Poi" par des femmes Maoris au village de Whakarewarewa (Rotorua).

A droite: Des jeunes guerriers Maori dansent la "Haka", la danse des guerriers des Maoris, en célébration du Traîté de Whaitangi.

Oben: Der traditionsgemäße Eingang zu einem Maori-Versammlungshaus in Te Kuiti, Region Waikato.

Rechts: Maori-Frauen führen einen Poi-Tanz im Whakarewarewa Village in Rotorua vor.

Oben rechts: Junge Maori-Krieger tanzen den Haka, den Kriegstanz der Maoris, anläßlich der Waitangi Treaty Feierlichkeiten.

Arriba: Entrada tradicional de un marae (sala de juntas Maorí) en Te Kuiti, Waikato.

Derecha: Danzarinas maories bailando con pois (pequeñas y ligeras bolas que penden de unas cintas y que son balanceadas al ritmo de la música, típico de danzas y ritmos maories) en Whakarewarewa Village, en Rotorua.

Arriba derecha: Jóvenes guerreros maories representando un haka (danza) en las festividades del Tratado de Waitangi.

Left: Native forest and stream at Rainbow Springs, Rotorua.

Above: Lake Okataina is one of several beautiful lakes in the Rotorua District known for their good trout fishing.

A gauche: La forêt de Nouvelle-Zélande et un ruisseau dans le parc de Rainbow Springs (Rotorua).

Ci-dessus: Le lac Okataina est l'un des plus beaux lacs de la région de Rotorua, fameux pour la pêche à la truite.

Links: Neuseeländischer Wald und Bachverlauf im Rainbow Springs Park in Rotorua.

Oben: Lake Okataina ist einer von mehreren idyllisch gelegenen Seen in der Umgebung von Rotorua, die für ihren Forellenreichtum bekannt sind.

Izquierda: Bosque nativo y arroyo en Rainbow Springs, Rotorua.

Arriba: Lago Okataina es uno de los varios maravillosos lagos en la Región de Rotorua conocida por la excelente pesca de la trucha.

Above: Sheep mustered prior to shearing in the central North Island near Raetihi.

Right: Papakorito Falls near Lake Waikaremoana in the Urewera National Park. Nearby is some of the finest podocarp forest in the country.

Ci-dessus: Des moutons rassemblés juste avant la tonte près de Raetihi dans le centre de l'île nord.

A droite: Les chutes Papakorito près du lac Waikaremoana dans le parc national d'Urewera. La forêt de Podocarpaceae de cette région, figure parmi les plus imposantes forêts de ce type en Nouvelle-Zélande.

Oben: Zusammengetriebene Schafe kurz vor ihrer Schur nahe Raetihi im Zentrum der Nordinsel.

Rechts: Die Papakorito Wasserfälle nahe beim Waikaremoanasee im Urewera Nationalpark. Der sich ganz in der Nähe befindende Podocarpaceae-Wald zählt zu den großartigsten Waldgebieten seiner Art in Neuseeland.

Arriba: Ovejas reagrupadas antes ser esquiladas en la zona central de la Isla Norte cerca de Raetihi.

Derecha: Las Cataratas de Papakorito (Papakorito Falls) cerca del Lago Waikaremoana en el Parque Nacional Urewera. Cercanos se encuentran algunos de los más hermosos bosques de coníferas del país.

Left: Spring at the Pukeiti rhododendron gardens on the eastern slopes of Mt Egmont.

Right top: Mt Egmont, 2,518m, looks out in all directions over rich dairy pasture.

Right bottom: Hill farms hard won from the "bush" inland of Tokomaru Bay, East Coast.

Links: Frühlingsstimmung in den Pukeiti Rhododendrongärten an der östlichen Hangseite des Mount Egmont.

Oben rechts: Der Mount Egmont, 2518 Meter hoch, überblickt das fruchtbare Weideland der Gegend in alle Richtungen.

Unten rechts: Diese auf Hügelland liegenden Farmen wurden dem dicht bewaldeten Gebiet der Tokomaru Bay an der Ostküste der Nordinsel entrungen.

A gauche: Les jardins de rhododendrons à Pukeiti sur le versant est du Mont Egmont au printemps.

En haut à droite: Le Mont Egmont, haut de 2 518 mètres, surplombe les pâturages très riches de la région.

En bas à droite: Ces fermes, situées sur des collines, ont été développées dans la région riche en forêts de Tokomaru Bay sur la côte est de l'île nord.

Izquierda: Primavera en los jardines de rododendros en las laderas orientales de Mt Egmont.

Superior derecha: Mt Egmont, 2.518 m, se divisa desde todas direcciones de los ricos pastos bovinos.

Derecha inferior: Colinas de granjas duramente ganadas al bosque en el interior de Tokomaru Bay, East Coast (Costa Este).

Above left: Model boat sailing in the Esplanade gardens of Palmerston North.

Left: The boat harbour at Gisborne.

Above right: Napier with its imposing Norfolk Island pine lined foreshore.

Right: A vineyard and modern house near Havelock North, Hawkes Bay.

En haut à gauche: Le modèle d'un bateau de Greenpeace à flot dans les jardins de l'Esplanade (Palmerston North).

A gauche: Le port de Gisborne.

En haut à droite: La ville de Napier, avec son impressionnante promenade bordée de pins de l'île de Norfolk.

A droite: Un vignoble avec une maison moderne près de Havelock North (Hawkes Bay).

Oben links: Modellboote segeln in den Anlagen der Esplanade Gardens in Palmerston North.

Links: Der Bootshafen von Gisborne.

Oben rechts: Die Stadt Napier mit ihrer eindrucksvollen, von Norfolk Island Kiefern gesäumten Strandpromenade.

Rechts: Ein Weingut mit modernem Wohnhaus in der Nähe von Havelock North, Hawkes Bay.

Arriba izquierda: Modelo de barco navegando en los Jardines Esplanade de Palmerston North.

Izquierda: El puerto pesquero de Gisborne.

Arriba derecha: Napier con su imponente paseo de pinos de Norfolk Island alineados a pie de playa.

Derecha: Viñedo y casa moderna próximos a Havelock North, Hawkes Bay.

94

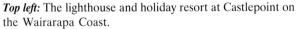

Top left: The lighthouse and holiday resort at Castlepoint on the Wairarapa Coast.

Left: The "Beehive" and House of Parliament in New Zealand's capital, Wellington.

Top right: The Wanganui River is rich in early Maori history and folklore.

Ci-dessus à gauche: Le phare et la station estivale de Castlepoint sur la côte de Wairapapa.

A gauche: Le fameux bâtiment du Parlement , le "Beehive" (ruche), et la Chambre des communes à Wellington, capitale de la Nouvelle-Zélande.

En haut à droite: La rivière Wanganui est riche en histoires et en folklores Maoris.

Ganz oben links: Der Leuchtturm und Erholungsort Castle-point an der Wairarapaküste.

Links: Der sogenannte "Beehive" (Bienenkorb) und das Parlamentshaus in Wellington, der Landeshauptstadt.

Oben rechts: Der Wanganuifluß weist einen Reichtum an frühgeschichtlichen Ereignissen und volkskundlichen Sagen der Maoris auf.

Superior izquierda: Faro y localidad de veraneo en Castle-point en la Costa de Wairarapa.

Izquierda: La "Colmena" y el Parlamento en la capital de Nueva Zelanda, Wellington.

Superior Derecha: El Rio Wanganui es rico en historia maorí y folklore.

Above: Wellington's cable car has carried commuters and shoppers up and down this steep hill since 1902.

Oben: Wellington – Seit 1902 fahren Pendler und Kauflustige mit der Seilbahn diesen steilen Berg hinauf und hinunter.

Ci-dessus: Le funiculaire de Wellington est utilisé comme moyen de transport pour se rendre en ville ou aller travailler depuis 1902.

Arriba: El teleférico de Wellington ha subido y bajado a pasajeros y compradores diariamente por este empinado cerro desde 1902.

This edition published in 1999 by New Holland Kowhai
An imprint of New Holland Publishers (NZ) Ltd
Auckland • Sydney • London • Cape Town

218 Lake Road, Northcote, Auckland 0627, New Zealand
Unit 1, 66 Gibbes Street, Chatswood, NSW 2067, Australia
86–88 Edgware Road, London W2 2EA, United Kingdom
80 McKenzie Street, Cape Town 8001, South Africa

www.newhollandpublishers.co.nz

Copyright © in photographs: Warren Jacobs with the exception
of the following images: page 27 (top) and page 62 (top),
Andrew Fear; page 64 (top), Sheena Haywood/Languages
International, page 65 (top), Bob McCree; page 94 (top),
Focus New Zealand Photo Library; page 96, Rob Suisted,
www.naturespic.com
Copyright © New Holland Publishers (NZ) Ltd

10 9 8 7 6

ISBN: 978-1-87724-621-0

Printed in China through Colorcraft Ltd., Hong Kong